Yijiun (Jenny) Lin, Author/ Illustrator
Chia-Ming Chang, Production Editor | Pei-Chi Su, Art Editor
Shiao-Shan Pan, Project Planning | Chun-Kuo Chia, Chief Editor
Shih-Yin Su, Associate Editor | Yi-Chiu Kao, Editor
Yijiun (Jenny) Lin, Cover Design | Taylor Fu, Proofreader
Li-Hsing Chang/ Ko-Yun Liao/ Yu-Tsai Xiao, Marketing Planning
Fei-Peng Ho, Publisher

Published
FLiPER Creative Inc.
6F, No. 112, Linsen N. Rd., Zhongshan Dist., Taipei City, Taiwan
Tel : (02)2562-0026 | Email : publish.service@flipermag.com

Issued
SBOOKER PUBLICATIONS
8F, No. 141, Sec. 2, Minsheng E. Rd., Zhongshan Dist.,
Taipei City 104, Taiwan
Tel : (02)2500-7008 | Fax : (02)2502-7676 | Email : sbooker.service@cite.com.tw

Taiwan Published
Cité Media Holding Group
2F., No.141, Sec. 2, Minsheng E. Rd., Zhongshan Dist.,
Taipei City 104, Taiwan
Customer Service line : 886-2-25007718 ; 886-2-25007719
24 hours Fax : 886-2-25001990 ; 886-2-25001991
Postal Transfer Acct : 19863813 (BOOKWORM CLUB CO., LTD.)
Service Email : service@readingclub.com.tw

Hong Kong Published
Cité Media Holding Group(Hong Kong)
193 Lockhart Road, Wanchai,
Hong Kong (Tung Chiu Commercial Centre 1F)
Tel : +852-2508-6231 | Fax : +852-2578-9337 | Email : hkcite@biznetvigator.com

Malaysia Published
Cité (M) Sdn. Bhd.
41, Jalan Radin Anum, Bandar Baru Sri Petaling,
57000 Kuala Lumpur, Malaysia
Tel : +603- 9057-8822 | Fax : +603- 9057-6622 | Email : cite@cite.com.my

ISBN : 978-986-5405-38-0

Printed in Taiwan
This edition first printing, December 2019
Selling Price NT$ 650

This publication is participated with"Graphic Art Design Project Support by
Department of Cultural Affairs, Taipei City Government".

Grandpa Santa

Written and illustrated by
Jenny Lin

Mercy, peace, and love
be multiplied to you.

Jude 1:2

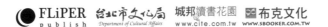

FLiPER publish　台北市文化局 Department of Cultural Affairs　城邦讀書花園 www.cite.com.tw　布克文化 WWW.SBOOKER.COM.TW

Once upon a time, there was a little girl called Amia, Santa Claus' granddaughter. Amia and Santa Claus lived on top of the Santa Claus Mountain in northern Finland.

Grandpa Santa was a workaholic. He started to prepare for Christmas Eve delivery long before December came. He was always busy and had no time to play with Amia. Instead, he gave Amia mountains of toys to play alone, but that didn't make Amia happy.

Lonely lonely Amia, all she wanted was to be with her Grandpa Santa.

The leaves were falling off the trees and the mountains were turning white. This year like all the other years, thousands of letters from children all around the world were flooding into Santa Claus' office. Santa Claus would read them, sort them out, make them into one final list and check if the addresses were correct.

The Christmas season was so hectic that he simply did not have time to be with Amia. Therefore Amia hated Christmas, and her one and only friend was Toby the talking teddy bear.

Lonely lonely Amia, all she wanted for Christmas was her Grandpa Santa to spend time with her.

The clocks were ticking and
Santa Claus was about to leave
for his Christmas Eve's delivery.
Amia and Toby sneaked into his
office asking for a bedtime story.

Izhevsk

"Grandpa, I really like the story about the baby reindeer and his first flying lesson. Could you read it to me before I go to bed tonight?" Amia asked Grandpa Santa.

"Amia dear, yes the baby reindeer is cute...oh what did you just ask me?" Grandpa Santa mumbled while he was busy getting ready to leave for the delivery.

"Could you read the reindeer story to me before I go to bed?" Amia asked Grandpa Santa again. "Oh I am so sorry, Amia! I don't have time for bedtime story now. How about I will read it to you tomorrow after my delivery?" Grandpa Santa replied.

Lonely lonely Amia, all she wanted for Christmas was bedtime story from Grandpa Santa.

"Let's go back to bed." Toby said to Amia.
Grumpy, angry, Amia did not want to go to bed.

"Knock! Knock!"

"Who would knock at this late hour?" Amia thought to herself. Spooky enough, the knocks were coming from her room.

"Hello, Amia!" When she opened the door she saw two Owls awaiting and greeting her by the windows of her room.

"We know a way to make you feel better." Grinned and said one of the Owls. "How about ruining Christmas? Have you heard of the Howling Forest and Robert? He could give you great advice." Said the other Owl.

Toby shivered when he heard the names "Howling Forest" and "Robert".

"No! Amia, Howling Forest...Robert...they are really scary." Toby whispered to Amia.

Amia thought since she hated Christmas, why not ruined Christmas altogether so no one could enjoy it? She decided to ignore Toby and follow the Owls into the Howling Forest.

Lonely lonely Amia, all she wanted for Christmas was to ruin it.

Into the dark magical forest the wind was howling like a sad tuba, but Amia was unafraid. "Ruining Christmas is the only way!" Amia said to Toby, and continued to move deeper into the dark dark woods.

The Owls stopped, the crows flew by and the moon lit its last glimpse of light onto the old gloomy tree, Juniper, where Robert the Wizard Owl resided. Robert was the embodiment of all things evil and destructive.

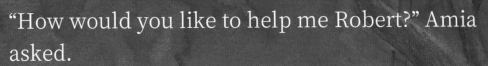

"How would you like to help me Robert?" Amia asked.

"I have an idea…" said Robert cunningly. "What if the children received something they dislike from your Grandpa Santa? Oh how they would be so disappointed, and so angry, just like how you are angry and disappointed with Christmas."

"It's a perfect plan! I know exactly what I should do!" Amia left the forest at once and dashed back to her home.

Lonely lonely Amia, all she wanted for Christmas was to ruin the joy of the season.

Sneaking into Santa Claus' bedroom, Amia took away his daily personal items such as his clothes, shoes, slippers, and many other things.

Amia went to the reindeers' stable, took out the huge gift bag from the sled and carefully opened all the gifts. She then swapped them with Grandpa Santa's old boring personal items and put them back into the gift bag.

That night, Grandpa Santa did not notice the gifts were being swapped, and he took off for his overnight delivery.

Amia stood by the window to see Grandpa Santa's sled going farther and farther, eventually it has gone out of her sight. Finally she closed her eyes for some good night sleep after a long day, and she couldn't wait for the morning to come.

Lonely lonely Amia, all she wanted for Christmas was to make the children cry when they saw their "new" gifts.

It was a beautiful Christmas morning, with the dawn set and the birds sang delightful songs up in the sky. Outside the house, the snow frosted every inch of the land, making it look crystal clear.

Amia woke up from her sound sleep. She gently washed her face, brushed her teeth and combed her hair.

After putting on her favourite pink dress and her soft leather boots, she turned to Toby and said, "It is a perfect day for a walk."

So they walked into the village, and she couldn't wait to see the sad faces of all the children.

When Amia and Toby were walking by the bright yellow house, they saw a few laughing kids who have just opened their Christmas gifts from Santa Claus.

"Look! I got a real Santa Claus hat!" One boy said joyfully.
"Good for you! I got a pair of gold-rimmed glasses. They are perfect." The girl said excitedly.
"Haha! Mine is the coolest! Santa Claus' painties!" The little naughty boy laughed.

Much to Amia's surprise, these children were enjoying their surprising gifts so much even though they were not what they had wished for. They were simply overjoyed to have received something from Santa Claus.

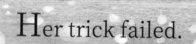

Her trick failed.

The winter has never been this cold. While the sea creatures under the thin ice of the Moonshine Lake were enjoying their Christmas swim freely and joyously, on top of it Amia felt numb and tears started to fall off her cheeks.

After his overnight delivery, Santa Claus finally got back home. He was so tired and he just wanted to get changed into his pajamas and go to sleep.

"Ouch!!" a huge pile of toys from the closet fell right into Santa Claus and overwhelmed him tremendously.

"Aren't these the toys I was supposed to deliver to the children?" Santa Claus was puzzled.

Amia did not want to go home. She was afraid that Grandpa Santa would punish her for what she had done. Toby, on the other hand encouraged her to go home and tell him the truth.

Grandpa Santa eventually figured out it was Amia who had pranked him and swapped the gifts. However, he also realized that while he was bringing happiness to other children, he neglected Amia and left her all alone even on Christmas.

Amia plucked up her courage and returned home.

"Grandpa, I am sorry to have pranked you and the little children. But Amia is lonely. All I want for Christmas is you being here with me." Amia said to Grandpa Santa.

Grandpa Santa felt an immense guilt after Amia told him her true feelings.
"Amia dear, yes all these years I travelled all over the world bringing happiness to other children, but what about my one and only granddaughter Amia?" Grandpa Santa sighed and gave Amia a real big bear hug. "I'm sorry grandpa…" cried Amia.
"My dear child, the guilt is mine too. Would you forgive grandpa and become my little helper bringing joy to the children together?" Grandpa Santa asked Amia.

Amia's eyes sparkled with tears and said, "Yes, I do. I want to be your helper. I want to make others happy the way you do!"

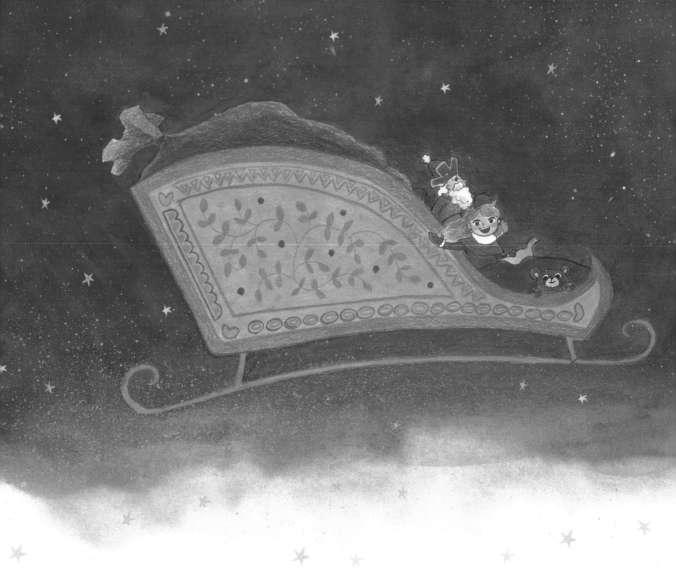

The following Christmas on a full moon night, Santa
Claus' reindeer became a little heavier carrying a brand
new helper, Amia. Grandpa Santa could tell his little
granddaughter as many bedtime stories and tales as she
wished while they were riding along together and
delivering gifts and joy to all the children around the
world.

Lovely Lovely Amia, all she learns about Christmas is simple:
Christmas is Peace; Christmas is Hope; and the biggest of all:

Christmas is Love.